# BLACK BOLD & BEAUTIFUL

Aurthor:
Jemema Thomas

Illustrator:
Afzal Khan

Acknowledgements

I would like to take this moment to first and foremost thank God for giving me this platform and opportunity to be able to write this book. Secondly, to my husband Quinson for always supporting any dreams I have and going above and beyond to help me to obtain such. To the ones who hold every part of my heart, my children, Jahquori,Qadejah and Jahquan, thank you for inspiring mommy to always be better. Not to be forgotten are my awesome parents Eliott and Lydia along with my best friend Jenell for always being my cheer leaders. To all my other family and friends to numerous to mention, you guys rock for always having my back with your constant support.

This book was inspired and dedicated to my beautiful daughter, my princess, Qadejah and all the little colored girls out there. Always remember, you are Queens and beautiful JUST the way you are.

Nicole Sanders had mixed feelings when her father said they were leaving their beloved home in Tortola, British Virgin Islands. Her father, Martin Sanders, had recently gotten a new job working as a construction engineer in a small Midwestern town known as Johns Creek, in the state of Missouri. She was very sad.

Nicole was seven years old and most of her friends in her elementary school were very unhappy about her leaving. As the day of her departure from Tortola drew near, Nicole tried everything she could to cheer herself up. She knew that moving to a new town and city meant that she would be making new friends, and most importantly, having new experiences and adventures.

In attempt to cheer her up, her father promised that she would go to a really nice school, have a brand new bedroom with new toys and make new friends. The promise of making new friends who were also tons of fun made Nicole quite happy!

As her father's car drove away from the streets of her old neighborhood, Nicole finally found herself looking forward to her new life.

The new house was bigger than the old one that they had back in Tortola. It was definitely not the ramshackle bungalow like her grand mother's house she often visited. Instead it was a beautiful two bedroom home with bricks on all four sides of the home, in a quiet street at the far end of the very small town.

The lawn was neatly mowed, and the little garden in front of the house was very beautiful. Nicole's new room in the house was a so much larger than her old one, and this gave her more space for her books and numerous new toys.

SCHOOL

As her father drove around the new town, Nicole noticed her new school. Even though she could only see its enormous grey gates, she couldn't help but get excited for her first day there.

Then, after settling in, with everything perfectly arranged by the movers, the entire family sat down and had a sumptuous dinner.

Later that night, after her father and mother went to sleep, Nicole tossed and turned restlessly in her bed. She could hardly sleep. All Nicole could think about was her first day at school and what it would turn out to be.

Thankfully, as she listened to the soft tick-tock of her bedside clock, she soon fell fast asleep, dreaming of her grand entrance into her new school.

"Hurry up, Mom!" said Nicole, "I don't want to be late." She was already dressed and ready for school. Nicole's mom smiled at her. "Hold on, Nicole. I'm trying to pack your lunch box."

Nicole just couldn't contain herself and became impatient. She just couldn't wait to get to school and start making new friends. She caught a brief reflection of herself in the side view mirror of her mother's car, average height, creamy chocolate skin and her thick hair, just like her father's.

The night before, her mother helped her weave her hair and decorated it with tiny beads of varying colors that made her look smart and elegant.

Her mother emerged, carrying Nicole's lunch box, which she handed over to her. The moment arrived, they were finally driving towards her new school. As her mother pulled up in the parking lot, Nicole saw all the other kids as they laughed and played. She couldn't wait to join them.

Before she could go to her new class, Nicole was taken to the principal's office. After all the necessary registration was done, the principal called in one of the teachers, who eagerly led Nicole to her new class as she waved goodbye to her mom.

Her new class teacher, Miss Reid, held Nicole's hand affectionately, and they both entered into a class at the far end of the hall. As soon as she was inside the class, Nicole knew that something was wrong.

Everyone was looking at her in wonder. Obviously, she was a new student, but it was even more visible that she was the only colored girl in the class. Nicole could see many of them whispering among themselves. Some of her new classmates were giggling and pointing at her, and this really made her blush with embarrassment.

"Good morning everyone," Miss Reid announced, "As you can all see, we have a new person here with us today. This is Nicole Sanders, and she recently moved to Johns Creek with her family. Everyone, now say hello to Nicole,"

"Hello Nicole!!!" they all chorused, and Miss Reid nodded with satisfaction.

Nicole only smiled shyly and lowered her face to the floor, looking at her feet. Miss Reid made her sit beside a boy with red hair whose name was Tommy. He didn't seem to pay any attention to her and went off to play with his other friends when their lunch break arrived.

Many kids formed circles in the school's playground at lunchtime and enjoyed their usual games but none paid attention to Nicole. She sat on an old bench in the corner of the playground, all alone, drawing small patterns in the white sand with a broken twig. At the other end of the playground, she could see two girls from her class pushing each other on a swing; oh how she wished it was her.

One of the girls, Susie, pointed at Nicole, and her friend Martha laughed. Susie had long auburn hair that flowed down to her shoulders like the mane of a pony, while Martha had black curly hair and deep blue eyes.

The girls walked towards Nicole and sat down on the bench beside her. At first, Nicole didn't notice their presence because she so focused on drawing her flower patterns in the sand, but Susie tapped her shoulder.

Nicole looked up and was very surprised to see the two girls while hoping to hear an invitation to be their friend and to play with them.

"You look very odd," said Susie, "How is it that your skin is so black?"
Nicole only stared at her, unable to find an answer to her question.

"Maybe she got burned by the sun," suggested Martha, "I think that's why her skin is as black as charcoal."

Still, Nicole remained silent.

Susie reached for Nicole's hair and grabbed a handful, "It feels strange. Why is your hair like wool? Is it hard to wash? Does it not hurt to keep such hair?"

Both girls giggled hard and left her alone in the playground and joined their other classmates. Nicole stood still, quite shocked at what happened. She hung her head low in sadness as tears welled up in her eyes and slowly walked back to the class at the end of her noon break. Nicole was so hurt and it showed on her face for the rest of her classes that day.

Sometimes, she sat in class staring longingly at Susie and Martha, wishing her hair was the same texture as theirs. She would say, "I wish my hair was as straight has theirs.  Why can't I have white skin and blue eyes?  I want to look like a movie star too!"

At the end of the school day, Nicole still felt very sad with no excitement from that long anticipated first day at school. She just couldn't get the beautiful images of Susie and Martha out of her mind. "Perhaps, they would want to play with me or be my friends tomorrow," she thought to herself.The ride back home was a long one.  Nicole was very quiet, despite her mom's many questions about her first day at school.

Nicole didn't eat much that night as is her norm, and her parents were quick to notice her sad countenance. Pushing away from the remnants of her half-eaten dinner, Nicole left the dining room and went back to her room. After a few minutes, she heard a soft knock on her door, and her mother poked her head in.

"Hey Nickie," her mother whispered, "mind if I come in?"

Nicole nodded her head, and her mother entered the room. She was lying down with her back turned to her mother.

"Is something wrong? I noticed that you have not talked about your first day at school. Didn't you like your new school or new friends?" her mother asked.

Nicole turned to her mother and asked, "Mom, is there a way for me to make my hair straight and silky? I want it to be like Susie's."

Her mother was a little shocked at her request. "No, Nicole. I think you're beautiful just the way you are; you don't need to look like them,"

She shook her head, "No, Mom. I want my hair to be like Susie's hair or Martha's hair!"

"Really?" asked her mother, "Is that what you really want?"

"Yes," said Nicole, happy that her mother was finally going to grant her request.

Her mother shrugged, "Okay, follow me. I have something to show you,"

Nicole followed her mother to the bathroom and waited for her mother to begin the process of turning her hair into something close to Susie's. Instead, her mother pointed at the large bathroom mirror nailed to the wall.

"Who is that?" her mother asked, pointing at Nicole's reflection in the mirror.

Nicole smiled, "That's me, and that's also you,"

"Good," said her mother, "Look at your beautiful dark skin, Nicole. You're as black as the panther. A symbol of strength and dignity. I know that you'll one day grow up to be the strong woman that I know you'll be. Also, look at your hair. It is as soft as sheep's wool; it represents how gentle and meek you can be."
Nicole only looked at her mother, too surprised to talk.

Her mother knelt down in front of her and put her hands on Nicole's shoulders and said, "There were great women in history who shared the same skin color as you. Their impact on the world will never be forgotten. Women like Rosa Parks, became known as the first lady of civil rights when she refused on principle to surrender her seat because of her race.

Women like Coretta Scott King stood firmly beside her husband, Dr. Martin Luther King, during the Civil Rights movement and refused to back down in the face of racial discrimination and intimidation. Women like Kamala Harris, the first black female vice president of the United States.

Nickie, many black women in history shared the same skin color as you and changed the world's history forever. Never let anyone tell you that you're not beautiful. Baby, you're Black, Bold, and Beautiful! You're a queen in the making, so never forget that.

I know that there will be times, like this one, when you will feel that you're not good enough; in those moments, remind yourself that you're a bold and beautiful black princess, perfect just the way you are! The world wouldn't be fun if we were all the same color. Each person is unique, just the way God intended."

A huge smile spread across Nicole's face and as she hugged her mom tightly, she said, "Thank you, Mommy."

"Promise me you will always remember that you are black, bold and beautiful."

"Yes, mommy. I promise." Nicole said, smiling at her reflection in the mirror.

The following day at school, Nicole was a lot happier. Beaming as she thought about her mother's words of inspiration. She didn't seem to mind her classmates ignoring her as they did yesterday. At lunchtime, she walked up boldly to Susie and Martha as the two girls played with the swing.

"Can I play with you?" Nicole asked.

Susie laughed, "Are you sure you can play with us in the sun? You don't think it will burn you too much?"

Nicole shook her head, "Susie, my darker skin actually helps protect me from the sun. I just have a different skin color from you, which makes me unique, just as your skin color does for you. My skin is as dark as the panther's, which makes me strong, and my hair is as soft as the sheep's wool, which makes me gentle. I'm just like you, only with a different skin color."

Both Martha and Susie looked at Nicole, too shocked to speak.

"Wow, your skin is really like a panther's?" Martha asked.

Nicole nodded her head, "Yes, that's what my Mom told me."

"That's totally awesome," Susie said in admiration.

After a few minutes, Martha said, "Would you like to play with us and our dolls after school, Nicole? I have a new collection that my mom got for my birthday."

"I'd like to," Nicole replied excitedly, "but I'll have to ask my mom first,"

They all giggled with excitement and played together until the lunch break was over.

By the end of the week, Nicole was friends with everyone in her class. A few weeks later, Miss Reid came into class with another black girl whose name was Sylvia. After being welcomed by everyone, Nicole introduced herself.

“Hello Sylvia, I’m Nicole,” she said.

“Hi Nicole,” Sylvia replied shyly.

“Want to play?” Nicole asked.

"Sure." Sylvia answered.

"Sylvia, guess what? We are Black, Bold and Beautiful just like many great and powerful women in history."

Both girls smiled with heads held high as they walked out of their classrooms.  At the noon break, all the girls played together as the bright rays of the sun illuminated their radiant, black and beautiful skins.

www.ingramcontent.com/pod-product-compliance
Ingram Content Group UK Ltd.
Pitfield, Milton Keynes, MK11 3LW, UK
UKHW061025310726
14090UKWH00023B/95

*9798538844302*